Dr. Kala

The Lost Book

Illustrated by
Ofir Corcos

To my inspiration,
Hila & Oriya

Published by Kalanit Ben-Ari, 2016

Text copyright © Kalanit Ben-Ari, 2016

Illustrations copyright © Kalanit Ben-Ari, 2016

Designed by Shani Barber Ivgi

Chapter One   5

Chapter Two   11

Chapter Three   19

Chapter Four   27

Chapter Five   31

Chapter Six   43

Chapter Seven   51

Chapter Eight   63

Chapter One

Lev is a 9 year old girl who loves books. In her room you can find books of all different sizes and colours! Anytime, anyplace you see Lev, there's a good chance she'll be reading a book. When Lev reads, she feels as if she has entered an imaginary world. There she meets new people, sees new places and goes on exciting adventures.

When mum goes to wake her up in the morning, she discovers Lev is already wide awake reading a book. Mum says, "Lev, it's time to brush your teeth now," and Lev says, "Soon, I just want to finish this paragraph". Then mum insists, "Lev it's time to get dressed now" and Lev answers, "Soon, I just want to finish this page".

After a while, dad says, "Lev it's time for breakfast now". Lev, who can hardly lift her eyes from the book, says, "Soon, I just need to finish this chapter". And when the family is driving to school, what do you think Lev is doing? You're right. She's reading her book!

One Monday morning, Lev was especially busy reading a story about a girl named Rona who has lost her beloved dog, Momo.

Mum saw that Lev didn't even notice what she was doing. As she brushed her teeth, got dressed and ate breakfast, her eyes did not once leave the book. Lev didn't even realise they had arrived at school!

Mum said, "It is time to go to class now. Have a lovely day and see you later". Three kisses, two hugs, one high five and mum left. This was their way of saying goodbye in the morning.

Chapter Two

Lev was curious about the book and just couldn't put it down. But then Mrs. Orla, her teacher, said "Lev, it's time to put the book inside your drawer now. We are learning maths".

Lev was just about to read what was going to happen to Rona and Momo. But this time she couldn't say, "Soon, I just want to finish the chapter", as Mrs. Orla was standing next to her waiting for her to put the book inside the drawer right now. So she did.

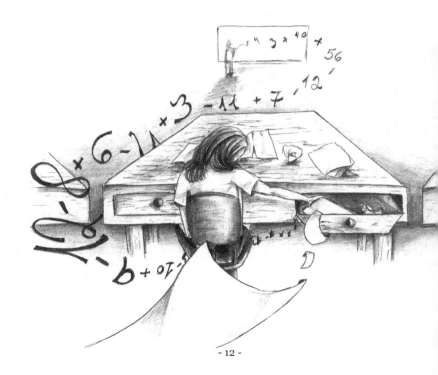

When the bell rang for a break, her best friend Ella suggested playing with the skipping rope in the school playground. Skipping rope was their favourite game. Then the school bell rang again and they rushed to art class. They were learning about the Egyptians and got to make their own 3D pyramids.

Next they went to lunch, and
one lesson seemed to pass after
another. Soon enough, the school
day was over. Lev saw her mum
waiting at the school
gate. Lev ran to
her mum, three
kisses, two
hugs, one high
five and mum
said with a

smile "How lovely to see you, I've missed you!" And together they went to the car to drive home.

Mum had just parked the car in front of their house when she heard Lev say in a panicked voice, "Oh no! I forgot the book at school!

We have to go back and get it!"

Mum said, "Ah dear! You wanted to finish the book today". Lev, with tears in her eyes said, "Yes! I can't wait! Let's go back!"

Mum considered the idea for a moment, but said, "Ah dear! I can see how much you want to go back to school.

Honey, it's too late now, it's almost time for supper. It will have to wait until tomorrow".

Chapter Three

Lev tried her best to change her mum's mind: "But mum, I have to know how the story ends! I can't wait until tomorrow!" Mum said, "Hmmm, I can see how disappointed you are to not be able to read the book. It's not a good time for me right now to go back to school so we will have to find another solution".

This is mum. Always saying there are other options. Sometimes it doesn't feel like that to Lev. But it didn't look like mum was going to change her mind so Lev kept quiet.

Mum said, "I can see how cross you are honey. You really wanted to finish this book today. It is frustrating not to know the end of the story. You know what? I will make us a cup of tea and we can

think about solutions".

What solutions? Lev thought, either I have the book and I'm happy or I do not have it and I'm sad. Lev and her mum sat down for tea and mum asked Lev about the book. So she told her about Rona, the girl with the long hair and a big smile who loves her dog Momo.

Rona received Momo as a present for her 2nd birthday and

now she is 10. Momo is a cheeky, lively dog who makes everyone laugh (Rona's friends find it especially funny when he dances on his two back legs). Momo is Rona's best friend.

When Rona is upset, Momo makes a sad face and walks on one leg until Rona laughs. When Rona is back from school, he runs and jumps up to lick her face. When Rona is ill, he comforts her with a furry hug. Rona feels like the luckiest girl in the world because she has Momo!

Chapter Four

One day, Rona took Momo for a walk in the park opposite her house. She stopped for a moment to look at the beautiful, golden leaves of the autumn. But then she realised that Momo was not by her side. Rona called out, "Momo, Momo, come back!" in all directions, but nothing! He didn't come back.

She called again and again, "Momo, Momo, where are you? Come back!". But there was no sign of Momo. Rona sat down under a tree and sobbed quietly to herself".

Mum: "And? How did it finish?"

Lev: "I don't know! That is when the teacher asked me to put the book down. I was so busy afterwards that I forgot about it. Now I don't know what happened!"

Mum: "Oh dear."

Lev and her mum sat quietly for a while. **Then Lev had an idea!!**

"Mum, maybe we can invent the end of the story", said Lev.

Mum: "What do you mean?"

Lev: "You, dad, Tom (Lev's big brother) and I can make up the ending to the story during supper".

Mum thought this was a great idea. So during dinner, Lev

repeated the story to dad and Tom
and invited them to make up their
own ending.

Chapter five

Dad wanted to go first. He said, "I think that because Momo is such a lovely dog, someone probably found him, thought that he was lonely and so took him home with them. Rona was very sad and cried a lot. She kept looking for him with her family. She didn't know Momo was missing her too and that he had a lovely new home.

Rona drew pictures of Momo, wrote him letters, and missed him a lot. The end."

Lev complained, "Dad! That is a very sad ending!"

But Dad said, "That is what I think might be the end".

"I hope not!" said Lev.

Tom couldn't wait any more

for his turn. He said, "I think that exactly one minute after Lev started crying under the tree, Momo came back to her all happy, licking her face and running around her as all dogs do. She hugged him, saying how worried she had been thinking that she might have lost him.

Then she attached his lead onto his collar so that she could be sure he wouldn't get lost again. And they lived happily ever after!" Tom finished with a proud look in his eyes.

Lev: "Oh, I like this ending!"

Mum was up next. "Wow. I don't think I can come up with another ending. You've used them all up!"

Lev insisted with a smile, "Mum, there are always more options".

"OK," said mum. "This is my ending: I think Rona called her family and friends and they all went to the park and searched for Momo. They split up, called his name and asked the people in the park if they had seen a medium

sized dog with fluffy white fur
and a cheeky face. They could
even show his photo on mum and
dad's mobile phones.

Just before sunset, all the family and friends met back up to discuss the next steps. But, as it started to get dark, they had to end the search for the day. Sad and concerned, they walked home thinking what they would be able to do in the morning. When they walked through the garden gate, they were surprised and thrilled to see Momo sitting near the door waiting for them!

Apparently he had lost Rona in the park, but could remember his way home. He had returned all by himself! Momo had been waiting for them the whole time they were looking for him! Rona hugged him and cried. But this time they were happy tears. They were all relieved and happy, and went inside for supper".

"Mum, that is an interesting ending!" said Lev.

Taking her time, Lev said, "OK, now it's my turn. I think that Momo was just playing hide and seek with Rona. He could see Rona crying from his hiding place. When he barked, Rona immediately recognised that familiar sound. She raised her eyes with a tiny smile and looked for him behind a bush. Momo was waiting for her with a wagging tail.

'Momo, I thought I lost you!' said Rona. Momo barked four times to say, 'I was just playing'.

Rona understood Momo's barks and said, 'OK, next time wait for me to say 'hide and seek 123' so we both know we are playing. And if I call, 'Momo please come now,' you need to come back to me so that I will know you are not lost'. Momo barked twice saying, 'OK, OK'.

And they went home happily ever after."

Dad was really impressed by the four stories. He said, "I can't wait to hear the real end of the story". After dinner, Lev noticed that she was no longer sad about forgetting her book. She went to sleep with excitement, thinking about the four possible endings. What was the real ending?

Chapter Six

The next day, mum woke Lev up. But this time there was no need to remind Lev to brush her teeth and get dressed. Lev jumped from the bed singing to herself, "Who let the dog out", went straight to brush her teeth and got dressed.

Then, to mum's surprise, Lev finished her breakfast early and was ready to go to school 20 minutes before the usual time! During school hours, she was too busy to read. But when dad came to pick her up from school, she didn't even say "Hi" and her eyes were already excitedly reading the book.

After a while, Dad asked, "So, what's going on?"

"Shhh, I'm reading!" interrupted Lev.

And after another little while, dad asked again, "So? What's the

end of the story?" and Lev replied, "Shhhhh... just a second. ... I finished the book!"

"And?" bursted Dad.

"You'll have to wait. I will tell you, mum and Tom during dinner" said Lev.

At dinner, Lev told them the end of the story: "Rona sat crying near the beautiful tree. She was devastated at the thought of losing her dog. She cried and cried until she had no more tears. But then, a small purple bird appeared in the sky and landed by Rona's side. The bird asked,

"Why are you crying?"

Rona was surprised that a bird could talk, but she was so upset she didn't give it much thought and just explained that she had lost Momo, her beloved dog.

The bird said, "I can help you find him". Rona rubbed her eyes with disbelief: "Really?? How??" The bird explained, "You can fly with me and see the park from above. It will be easier for you to spot Momo from up there."

"But I don't have wings!" said Rona.

" I can make you fly. I'm a magic bird. That's why I can talk too! I can do things that no other bird can!" replied the bird.

"OK. Let's try," said Rona.

"All you need to do is to close your eyes and say twice 'I need wings to find Momo', said the bird.

So that's exactly what she did -

"I need wings to find Momo.
I need wings to find Momo."

But nothing happened.

Chapter Seven

Rona opened her eyes and looked at the bird with a questioning expression. The bird said, "Look behind you". Rona didn't feel a thing but, when she looked behind her, she saw two stunning, colourful wings! "Wow, this is cool", thought Rona. She tried to fly but it looked as if she was just jumping. "You have to keep practicing and it will come," said the bird with confidence. So she did! The jumps got higher and higher until she could skip in the air.

And the skips became higher and higher until she could fly for a metre. And the metres went further and further until she could fly across the whole park. Higher and higher above the trees. It was fun. It was beautiful. It was peaceful. She felt as light as a feather in the air.

From far above, she could see many people in the park— she saw families playing together or having a picnic; adults juggling and cycling, children playing football and others just relaxing on the grass. She flew around in circles, looking very carefully for Momo. Rona saw many dogs in the park, but she could not recognise her Momo.

She was looking and looking, and just before she was about to give up, she saw something familiar! The lower she flew, the closer she came. A blob became an animal. An animal became a dog. A dog became a cheeky face with fluffy fur. She could definitely recognise this dog- it was the one and only Momo!!

And he was not alone!! Playing with him was a small, cute, female dog, with white fur and brown spots. Momo and the other dog looked so happy together, chasing each other's tails, rolling over in the grass and barking happily.

Rona couldn't wait any more and landed next to them. As soon as Momo saw her, he ran towards her to give Rona her usual happy welcome of jumping and licking her face.

"Where have you been Momo?? I was so worried about you!" said Rona. Momo barked to say, "I met a nice friend and didn't realise I was lost!"

His new friend hid behind

Momo, shyly watching Rona. Rona reached out her hand to stroke her.

Rona could see how much Momo liked his new friend. She also saw that there was no collar on the dog to identify who she belonged to.

"Do you have a family?" asked Rona. The dog shook her head sadly. "Would you like to come with us?" suggested Rona. "Woof Woof!" barked the dog happily.

"Great", said Rona. She added, "Is it ok if we call you Mami?"

"Woof Woof", barked Mami happily.

Rona could see the purple bird watching from a distance. She thanked her for her help. The bird flew higher in the air. When Rona looked behind her, there was no evidence of her wings! How strange is that, she thought to herself.

Rona took Momo and Mami

and walked home. And they lived happily ever after."

"That was quite an adventure!" said Tom.

"I'm not sure which ending I like the most," said Mum.

"And that was the end?" asked Dad.

Rona, who didn't really want to finish this adventure, added, "Not really..."

"So... how did it end?" they all said at the same time.

Lev said, "It ended with, 'They lived happily ever after, until one day....'"

Chapter Eight

Printed in Great Britain
by Amazon

18587160R00045